Bella Sara™

10

Shamal's Secret

HarperFestival is an imprint of HarperCollins Publishers.

Bella Sara #10: Shamal's Secret
Cover and interior illustrations by Heather Theurer
Copyright © 2010 Hidden City Games, Inc. © 2005–2010 conceptcard. All rights reserved.
BELLA SARA is a trademark of conceptcard and is used by Hidden City Games under license.
Licensed by Granada Ventures Limited.
Printed in the United States of America.
For information address HarperCollins Children's Books, a division of HarperCollins Publishers,
10 East 53rd Street, New York, NY 10022.
www.harpercollinschildrens.com
www.bellasara.com

Library of Congress catalog card number: 2009932797
ISBN 978-0-06-168789-1
10 11 12 13 14   CG/CW   10 9 8 7 6 5 4 3 2 1
❖
First Edition

Bella Sara™

10

Shamal's Secret

Written by Felicity Brown
Illustrated by Heather Theurer

HARPER FESTIVAL
An Imprint of HarperCollinsPublishers

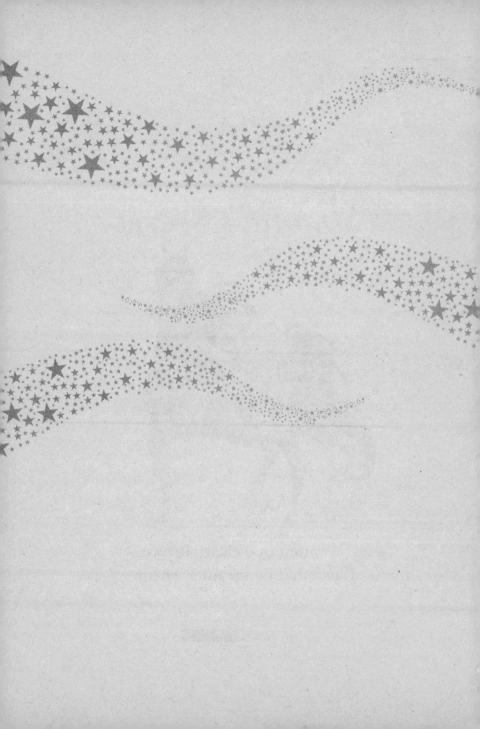

1

Amber's whole body felt like it was twitching with energy. *I'm not nervous*, she insisted to herself as she stared out over the arid landscape below her window. With a growing feeling of excitement and dread, Amber realized it was finally time for her to leave the small dwelling she shared with her parents and begin her Year of Grace. *This is the most important day of my life, she thought.*

Amber had been preparing for this day for months. If she were chosen today by the mysterious Desirée, Amber would go with them to their home in Cavern-est. There, she would work hard for the next year, doing anything the Desirée asked of her. In return, she could only hope they would offer her the honor of joining their ranks.

The Desirée, a mysterious society of desert women, were much loved in Autumn Sands, the region where Amber had lived all her life. The Desirée had a special bond with the desert, and with dune lupines, the beautiful, wolflike crea-tures that protected Autumn Sands.

Amber had seen the Desirée before, when they had traveled to her hometown of Medab in the past to col-lect girls to begin their own Years of Grace. Amber couldn't imagine what it would feel like to become one of them. If she were allowed to stay on at the end of the year, Amber would bond with a dune lupine cub and begin her training to become one of the Desirée.

Ever since she was a little girl,

Amber had wanted to join the Desirée. Still, she knew the Year of Grace would not be easy—the days would be long, and the work would be hard. A tiny part of her was worried that she knew little about what the Desirée really *did* in their home city of Cavernest. What would Amber be asked to do? What challenges would the next year bring?

Amber felt a squeeze on her shoulder. She turned to see her mother, Kyran, wiping tears from the corners of her eyes as she smiled down at her daughter. "Are they here?" Kyran asked. "Have they arrived yet?"

Amber shook her head. "Not yet, Mother."

Kyran stroked Amber's hair and gazed out the window with a faraway look in her eyes. "This year will change you forever, Amber," she said wistfully.

Amber jumped up suddenly, bumping her mother's hand away. "Mother," she said with excitement, "I see them. They're here at last!"

As she looked at the scene below the window, Amber's heartbeat quickened. Twelve beautiful women appeared, their flowing red silk dresses licking the air like flames. Next to the women strolled their dune lupines—the cubs they had each been given after their own Years of Grace. The dune lupines looked powerful but graceful as they made their way into Medab.

"Quickly!" Kyran cried, pushing her daughter forward. "You must go to the town square to meet them!"

By the time Amber and Kyran got to the center of town, three other girls were already lined up for the Desirées' inspection. Amber felt a flash of panic. She knew she should join the line, but she didn't want to leave her mother. Amber didn't know how long it would be before she saw her again. "Go, Amber," said Kyran softly. She touched Amber's shoulder, and Amber knew that her mother could sense how torn she felt.

She turned, gripping Kyran's arm as she felt tears form. "Mother!"

But her mother simply stroked her cheek reassuringly. "Don't be afraid, Amber," she said gently. "You are ready. You know you will always be with me in my heart."

Amber blinked back her tears as she looked into Kyran's warm, sure eyes. "I *am* ready," she whispered, knowing it was true.

Then things began to happen quickly. Amber's mother was pulled back into the crowd, and Amber took her place beside Myri, a small, gentle girl who lived in a dwelling above Amber's. Myri gave her a small smile, and Amber nodded and turned to face the Desirée, who were now standing before the girls.

Up close, the Desirée were more stunning than Amber had imagined. Their long hair was pinned up in a formal style, and their eyes gleamed with the wisdom of ages. Beside them, the dune lupines seemed to glow from within, their fur shining with streaks of bronze and silver.

One woman stood out in a dress the color of a brilliant desert sunset. Her eyelids were painted with sparkling sand that seemed to make her eyes glow with light. *She must be the leader*, thought Amber, as the woman turned her gaze upon her.

"You are Amber Murin," the woman said.

Amber nodded, wondering how this powerful Desirée knew who she was, before getting hold of herself and forcing out the words, "Yes, I am."

The woman turned to the crowd. "I am Yris, a leader of the Desirée. Who freely gives this girl to us so she can begin her Year of Grace and learn the truth of the desert, the ways of dune lupine, the evil of the Equine, and the mysteries of the universe itself?"

Beaming with pride, Kyran stepped from the crowd. "I do," she said.

The woman turned back to Amber. "Amber Murin," she said, in a low, serious voice, "for the next year, you are a servant of the Desirée."

Amber swallowed and took a deep breath. This was really happening. She could do this.

Medab was the first stop on the Desirée's journey through Autumn Sands. They would continue through the desert, stopping in villages along the way to choose more girls for the Year of Grace. As well as Amber, the Desirée selected two other girls from Medab—Myri and a chatty girl named Ruby. For Amber, Myri, and Ruby, being the first to be picked up meant a long journey through the desert with plenty of time to think about what may await them in Cavernest.

Amber knew about Cavernest, of course, although she had never traveled there. It was the home city of the Desirée and it was well known for the beautiful blue glass, Cavernglass, produced there. Cavernest was created when a huge meteor struck the desert, forming a large crater. The heat from the impact was so intense, it had fused the blue summer sand into glass, creating a blue crystalline crater bowl. The meteor also created a natural spring at the bottom of the crater. With its beautiful blue lake within a blue glass crater, and many dwellings and ramps carved into the glass showing through to the bright blue bedrock, Cavernest was said to be the most beautiful place in Autumn Sands.

Amber was eager but also nervous to get there. As they made their way through new villages, more young servants of the Desirée joined their ranks until Amber felt as if she were one of an army. She estimated there must be fifty other girls in her company.

The journey through the blue

summer sands was hot and tiring. In Autumn Sands, the color of the desert changed with each season. In autumn the sands were red, becoming white in winter, green in spring, and blue in summer. As she battled the heat, Amber found herself wishing for the lush green of spring or even the pure cool of winter.

The nights were also long, and Amber missed her parents terribly. To pass the time, Amber would sometimes make small talk with Ruby, but she found it hard to get out of the conversation. "Don't you think? Don't you find that . . . ?" Ruby would pester her about the tiniest things, until Amber would finally roll over and pretend to be asleep.

On the third day, Amber was trooping along when Myri gasped and pointed. "Look!" she said.

Amber squinted as she peered toward the horizon where Myri was pointing. At first, she could only make out a huge dust cloud flowing over the desert. But as the cloud moved closer, Amber could see the red garments of other Desirée! The dune lupines next to Amber and Myri began grunting and barking in excitement.

"Oh, my," Myri whispered suddenly, sucking in her breath. "What is *that*?"

Amber tried to see what her friend was talking about. She could now make out the telltale weapons and leather armor of the Desirée warriors. And there, in the middle—

Amber gasped. *Could it be?*

She felt herself shaking as the warriors came closer. They were dragging along a huge beast. It was many times larger than a dune lupine, and it snorted and rolled its eyes wildly. Strong ropes held the beast in check, and the Desirée warriors still seemed to struggle to control it, tugging and pulling the huge creature along.

The Desirée warriors stopped several

yards away, and a few of them walked up to Yris, who had ordered Amber and the other girls to stay back. Amber was glad; she felt frozen with fear at the sight of the huge beast. She wasn't sure she could keep moving forward even if she wanted to.

As murmurs passed between the warriors and the Desirée at the front of the procession, the girls buzzed with whispers and excitement.

"What are they saying?" Amber heard Ruby ask, as a girl from another town hissed, "They say they're joining our procession to Cavernest!"

Amber tried to swallow, but her mouth was too dry. *Joining our procession?* She felt a chill all over. How could she be expected to travel with . . .

"The beast, too?" Myri asked, glancing over at it fearfully.

The girl turned to Myri and smirked, although Amber could tell she was trying to hide her fear. Beneath her tunic, she was shaking.

"The beast has a name," the girl replied, shaking her head. "It's a *horse*."

A horse. Amber felt her heart beat wildly.

It was as if all her worst fears were coming true.

2

The night before Amber had been given to the Desirée, she and her mother had lain close together on their sleeping pillows, watching the stars through a narrow window near the roof of their dwelling. While neither one of them said it, Amber knew they were both too restless to sleep. Amber was nervous about her Year of Grace and what her time with the Desirée would bring. Her mother also seemed lost in her own world.

Finally, Amber's mother had broken

the silence. She had turned to face her daughter, her eyes warm even in the moonlight. "You must be very brave this year, Amber," she said. "The Desirée are very important to the people of Autumn Sands. They protect us and it will be an honor for you to spend a year with them."

"I know," Amber had said. Ever since she could remember, people had told her how important the Desirée were to their desert existence, how wise and powerful.

"Their ability to communicate with the dune lupine is very important to all of us," her mother continued. "It is our bond with the lupine that keeps us safe. Without them, our lands would have been overrun by horses centuries ago."

Amber had breathed in sharply. *Horses.* Since she was a little girl, she had been taught that horses were evil, violent, greedy creatures. She had never seen one in person, but she knew they were very large compared to the dune lupine, and she imagined huge, dark, fanged creatures with wild eyes and a stench of blood.

"You know the dune lupine fought a long war in the past," her mother had added. "Now the Desirée care for and protect the dune lupine so that the lupine can continue to keep our villages safe from horses."

Amber didn't reply. She was imagining dune lupines fighting with terrifying horse creatures, teeth gnashing and flesh tearing. She'd wondered if she would come across a horse in her time with the Desirée. Just the thought had sent icy prickles down her spine.

"Mother," Amber had said after a few minutes, "why are horses evil?"

"It is in their nature to destroy," her mother had replied with a sigh. "They bring the storms, hunger, and thirst. The Thunder Horse from legend gallops through the sky making storms that strike the land. You must beware of them, Amber, because they possess the lure of the equine. They are evil, violent monsters, but if you look into their eyes, they may charm you into believing that they are good and true. Then, once they've gained your trust, they will destroy you."

Frightened, Amber had gathered her blankets around her, trying to fight the chill that had taken over her body. *I hope I don't see a horse during my Year of Grace,* she had thought fiercely, feeling sleep move even farther from her grasp.

The first night the horse was in the camp, Amber huddled close to the fire she shared with several other girls. As she ate her bread and meat, she thought back to the conversation she'd had with her mother the night before she had joined the Desirée. Eventually Amber's curiosity got the better of her fear, and she snuck a glance at the huge horse that was tied by hundreds of ropes to a stake in the ground several yards away.

Amber tried not to stare, but she couldn't help it. The horse was huge and terrifying—at once just like and very different from what she'd imagined. His large, shiny body was strong and lean. He had a long, thick neck that led to a stretched-out, almost boxy face. Shining, intelligent dark eyes were set deeply near the top of his head. His mouth sat below flared nostrils, and every so often he would let out a startling "*Naaayy!*" that revealed a neat row of large white teeth. Small ears sat on the top of his head, and a mane of glossy hair grew all the way down his neck, creating a sort of flag that he shook and waved every time he moved his head. Even in his tight restraints, he seemed defiant. He tossed his head and snorted angrily, and his eyes, which shined in the dark night, seemed to glare at the girls.

The horse was so large, it was

impossible not to be scared of him. *But at the same time . . .* Amber bit her lip, not wanting to finish the thought. She couldn't help it, though. *He's beautiful.* Amber felt a shudder run down her spine, feeling like a traitor. *Maybe that's what makes horses so dangerous,* she thought. *They're so beautiful, they lull you into thinking they can't be as evil as they are!*

It touched Amber's heart to see the huge animal struggle, and, for a moment, she almost felt sympathy for him. But then she shivered, imagining the powerful creature trampling their camp and all the girls in her company. *It is in his nature to destroy,* she reminded herself.

As the girls finished up their dinner, Ruby caught Amber openly staring at the beast. When Ruby caught Amber's eye, she smirked. Then, as if reading Amber's thoughts, she said, "Don't be fooled by his appearance. Horses truly are evil. Have you heard the story of the horse that burned Ilnut, for example?"

Amber shook her head.

"Long ago, the people of the small village of Ilnut lived a quiet but prosperous life," Ruby began. "The main trade in the village was making paper from the leaves of the rare wyla tree, which grew easily in Ilnut, because it is close to an oasis. One day, one of the men of the village was collecting wyla leaves to be pressed into paper when he came across a huge, terrifying horse drinking from the oasis. Suddenly, the man had a vision: the entire village of Ilnut, engulfed in flames!"

The girls around Amber gasped.

"It was a mind picture," Myri whispered from beside Amber. "Horses have the power to put images in your head. It's part of the lure of the equine."

A murmur went through the crowd, and Ruby continued:

"The man was terrified, but when

the vision ended, he was alone at the oasis. The horse was gone, and the man thought that perhaps he'd been day-dreaming the whole time. Horses were rarely seen in that part of Autumn Sands, so he figured he must have imagined the whole thing."

"He didn't, though, did he?" whispered Uli, a young girl who had joined their procession several towns after Medab.

Ruby shook her head, clearly enjoying the attention. "No," she replied. "On his way back to town, the man spot-ted the remains of a pack of kangaroo rats, trampled to nearly nothing. It was then that he heard an unearthly sound, like a roll of thunder rumbling through the desert! *Pa-rump pa-rump pa-rump.* Looking ahead at the village entrance, he saw the horse he had seen at the oasis, along with five or six others!"

Amber gasped.

"The man watched in shock as the

horse from the oasis opened his terrible mouth and breathed fire into the village of Ilnut!"

Myri shivered. "Oh, no . . ."

Ruby nodded. "Oh, yes. And because the desert air was so dry and windy—and because the town was filled with dried paper—it was only a matter of minutes before Ilnut burned to the ground. Just as it had in the man's vision."

Amber bit her lip, glancing over at the horse-beast. She imagined licks of flame coming from its mouth.

"What happened to the man?" Uli spoke up finally, her voice quaking with fear.

Ruby seemed startled, as if she had forgotten that part of the story. "Oh, the man. Well, he wandered in the desert for days before coming upon a pack of Desirée and their dune lupine companions. Once the Desirée heard what happened, they organized a hunting pack and cornered the band of horses as they were traveling from Ilnut to Cavernest." Ruby paused, smiling nastily. "There wasn't much left of the horses once the dune lupines were done."

Amber sighed, trying to quiet the fear that gripped her body. But it was no use. Horses were made to destroy, and for the first time in her life, she was in the presence of one of the terrifying creatures.

Ruby stood then, and gradually, the other girls followed her lead, wandering from the campfire and drawing closer to the horse. None of them was brave enough to get closer than four or five yards away.

Ruby looked back at Amber, Myri, and Uli. "I dare you to get closer," she taunted.

Amber shook her head.

"What?" Ruby asked. "Are you scared?" She herself took a step closer and then jumped high in the air when the horse let out a loud snort.

"Ha!" Amber cried, unable to stop her laughter. "You're not so brave, Ruby."

Ruby scowled at Amber and then glared at the horse, who was still struggling with the ropes. "Stupid horse!" She kneeled down in the sand, picking up a small but sharp piece of glassy stone. Without another word, she pulled her arm back and threw the rock at the horse with all her might. The horse let out a sharp, furious cry as the rock cut into the flesh of its shoulder. His eyes shined brighter in the dim light, lit now by the fire of anger. He snorted again, a quick, brash sound that sounded to Amber like a challenge.

"Serves you right!" Ruby shouted, folding her arms. "That's for everything you horses have done to Autumn Sands." She turned to the other girls, her eyes large and commanding. "If you're loyal to the Desirée and the dune lupine," she instructed, "pick up a rock and do what I just did. Make him feel the pain his kind have caused us!"

Amber took in a sharp breath. *Make him feel pain?* As the girls around her kneeled down, searching for rocks, Amber felt a stirring deep in her heart. Rocks began flying toward the creature, and it snorted angrily, tearing at its ropes to try to get away—but it was impossible. The beast could barely move.

Amber stepped into the line of fire and held up her hand. "Stop!" The word left her lips before she even knew what she was saying.

"What do you mean, 'stop'?" Ruby demanded. "This is a *horse*, Amber. The enemy of the Desirée and all that follow them!"

Amber paused. She glanced back at the animal, and was stunned to see him looking directly at her, warmth in his liquid brown eyes. *Thank you,* he seemed to be saying. Amber felt her mouth drop

open, staring at the beast, but she quickly turned away.

"He may be a horse," Amber said, "but he's already our captive. If the Desirée haven't chosen to hurt or kill him, why should we?"

The girls grumbled in response, but they all seemed to see the wisdom in Amber's words. Soon they were called back to the main fire for the night's entertainment, and the moment with the horse seemed to be forgotten.

As they walked, Amber felt Myri suddenly step in beside her, take her hand, and squeeze it. "He's kind of . . . beautiful, isn't he?" Myri whispered to her, too quietly for the other girls to hear.

Amber glanced at the others to make sure no one was watching and then nodded quickly. "It's as if . . . ," she said softly, "as if he knows me, almost."

Myri looked thoughtful. "He's so powerful," she said. "I've heard stories of horses with wings, but I saw none on him."

Amber nodded again. "It almost makes me wonder . . . if . . . if . . ." *If there could be any good in horses,* she wanted to say. The beast hadn't looked dangerous or evil when they'd drawn close to it. His eyes had looked so grateful when Amber had stopped the girls from throwing the rocks. Could he be . . .

But then Amber stopped herself with one thought: the lure of the equine! Of *course* looking into the horse's eyes had made her question whether or not he was evil. That was part of the horse's dangerous magic, and she had almost played right into it!

"If . . . the Desirée *should* just kill him," she finished in a louder voice, giving Myri a look. "Horses are dangerous and evil, Myri. End of story."

Myri looked as though she had been slapped. She slipped away from Amber and refused to look at her for the rest of the night.

Back at the main campfire, the Desirée performed a ribbon dance to celebrate life. Amber found herself entranced by the twirling, shining red ribbons and by the rhythmic walk of the dune lupines who rolled and wove in and through the dancers. She didn't even think about the horse again until bedtime.

As she walked away from the fire, Amber couldn't resist taking one last glance at the horse. When she was within a few yards, though, she heard fierce whispering. Two of the Desirée were standing near the horse, deep in conversation.

"I just don't know," said one of the women, a silky-haired blonde. "We risked so much to capture this horse, the mighty Shamal. Three warriors wounded; one lost her life. It's hard to imagine that he's worth the sacrifice."

Amber was shocked. *Worth the sacrifice?* They hadn't merely captured the horse in battle, they had sought him out!

The other Desirée, a striking brunette, agreed. "I wonder if Shamal is as magical as they say," she whispered. "Can he really solve our problems with his so-called 'horse magic'?"

The blonde nodded. "And is it right for us to stoop to using a horse in the first place?"

The two spoke for a bit more, but in murmurs so low that Amber could no longer make out their words. Finally, they broke away and headed to the sleeping area. Amber glanced at the horse one more time, wondering what magic this beast could possibly possess that would be strong enough for the Desirée to take a chance on their mortal enemy. The horse caught her eye again, his intense brown gaze almost pulling her in, but she quickly looked at her feet and scurried away to bed.

* * *

Some time later, Amber awoke to the chilly breezes and mysterious sounds of the desert night. As she stared up at the millions of tiny stars shining brightly overhead, Amber was gripped by a sudden vision. An image of a coiled rope appeared in her mind.

She frowned. Had she been dreaming? What sort of trick was her brain playing on her? Her head began to tingle and itch, and then it came again: *rope!* She sat up, and her eyes were drawn to the horse-beast.

Amber slowly slipped out from beneath her blankets. She wanted to resist, to roll over and go back to sleep, but the image of rope kept coming, again and again. As soon as she was standing, Amber looked over at the beast, Shamal.

He was staring right back at her. Amber's feet seemed to be moving without her consent as she drew closer and closer to the horse.

Rope, her mind insisted. *Rope. Rope.* And as she got closer to Shamal, the image in her mind changed, and suddenly she was no longer seeing a coiled rope. Instead, she saw one of the carefully tied ropes that held Shamal. It almost seemed to be disappearing into his skin.

Amber drew close to the horse—closer than she ever thought she'd dare—and saw the rope from her vision digging sharply into Shamal's shoulder.

What am I doing? she wondered, as her hands moved forward to grasp the rope that was causing the horse pain. *This is a horse! This is our enemy! Move away!* But she couldn't.

Amber began loosening the knot that held the rope in place. *I'm not setting him free,* she told herself, *just giving him a bit of relief.* She felt like this was something she was compelled to do, whether or not she wanted to.

Carefully, Amber loosened the rope and then formed a new knot. Just as she was pulling it tight, a voice cut through the still night air, making Amber jump. "What are you *doing*?!"

CHAPTER

3

It was Myri. And as soon as the words were out of her mouth, the spell was broken. Amber dropped her hands to her sides, but already the camp seemed to be stirring to life. Almost immediately, the dune lupines began to bark. It was as if they could sense that something was amiss. Amber felt her heart sink at the sound of their howls.

The dune lupines. I have betrayed them.

When Amber finally gathered her senses, she looked up to find herself surrounded by the Desirée.

"What happened?" demanded Yris. Her voice was brisk, but not angry. Still, Amber felt tears forming behind her eyes.

"I . . . I . . . I'm not sure," Amber stammered.

Yris turned to her fellow Desirée, and a look passed between them—Amber couldn't believe it, but it looked like mercy. Yris moved closer to her, placing a warm hand on her shoulder. "It is all right, child," she said in a low voice, her clear eyes boring into Amber's. "The horse got into your mind. It charmed you."

Amber swallowed. It was the truth. She realized she *hadn't* been in control of herself. If she had been, she would never have helped a horse! She was terrified of horses! Before Amber could say anything, Yris shouted for the other girls to join them, and soon the whole camp was gathered around Amber.

"You must beware the horse's powerful magic," Yris instructed the girls, making a warning gesture toward the silent beast. "Horses are dangerous, hateful, and evil, but they possess a powerful magic—it is known as the lure of the equine. Give them the tiniest bit of attention, and they will charm you. They'll convince you that horses are good, and it is wolves and the Desirée who are evil! Before you know it, the horse will turn on you, and many people will lose their lives."

Amber shivered. She hated to think what may have happened if Myri hadn't woken and trailed her to the horse. What she had almost done was dangerous . . . and yet . . .

She bit her lip and chanced a quick glance at the horse. It stared back without hesitation, regarding her with huge, dark, curious eyes.

It didn't feel evil, she realized. The image of the rope in her head hadn't been uncomfortable, hadn't hurt her at all. In fact, *it felt natural.* Amber stared the beast in the eyes, feeling a strong pull. *As natural as breathing air . . .*

Amber gasped, pulling her eyes away. *The lure of the equine!* Yris was still lecturing the girls, and nobody seemed to notice Amber was not paying attention.

For the rest of the lecture, the rest of the night, and well into the next day, Amber wouldn't allow herself to glance even briefly at the horse.

It's not natural, she told herself, as she settled back in the sleeping area that night. *Not natural at all!*

The next day, Amber wondered what was wrong with her. She knew that it was a privilege to be chosen for a Year of Grace and that she was lucky to be traveling through the desert with the powerful Desirée. But the long trek had started to feel like a huge burden.

I didn't get much sleep last night.

I must just be tired, Amber told herself. In her heart, though, Amber knew that the problem was deeper than tiredness. What Amber felt was big and unsettling, coloring her view of everything she saw. As the day grew longer and hotter and brighter, Amber felt more than tired, she felt . . .

. . . *wrong.*

But what did that even mean? Everything she had ever been taught told her that this was the most amaz-ing part of her life so far. The Desirée had accepted her and even forgave her for what had happened with Shamal the night before.

But what do they know?

Amber shuddered. What was she thinking?

And the horse. She could sense it behind her, plodding along, tired. Sha-mal's ropes had been retightened, and he was being led by a group of the strongest Desirée warriors. Amber had avoided looking at him all day, but the pull was now becoming hard to ignore.

She turned, meaning only to give him a quick glance.

Shamal's brown eyes locked on hers, boring into her. Amber let out a breath, feeling beaten. It was like Shamal could see *inside* her—down to the bottom of her very soul. And she knew, somehow, he didn't like what he saw. She had disappointed him.

Amber struggled to pull her gaze away. Why did she care? *Who cares what a horse thinks?*

She struggled forward, but each step felt like a chore. She swore this was the hottest day of her time with the Desirée; the sun bore down on the procession, and there wasn't even a hint of a breeze to relieve their suffering. The air was oddly still and silent, too, as though the desert were waiting for something.

Wrong, Amber couldn't help thinking, shaking her head as she trudged forward. *It all just feels wrong.*

Suddenly, a sharp sound broke the silence, first in the distance, but then hurtling toward them with startling speed. *Whooooooooooosh.* Looking up, Amber was stunned to see a wall of sand moving toward the procession! The desert before them quickly disappeared as the whirling cloud of red sand came closer and closer, transforming everything in its path.

"Sandstorm! Everyone take cover!" Yris shouted.

The girls scattered, confused; there was no cover to take. This part of the desert was completely bare: The landscape consisted of sand, sand, and more sand, without even a village or a tree to offer shelter. Amber struggled to bring her clothing over her face, but as the wall of sand came over her, it felt as if she were being stung by a million tiny hornets. Grains of sand pelted her body, and she twisted and turned, trying to protect herself, to get out of the wind, but there was nowhere to go.

"*Auugsh!*" Amber heard screaming as the girls were covered by the storm. Worse, she heard screaming from the Desirée themselves. Even the sisterhood was helpless.

The wind was strong enough to knock Amber off her feet, and she crouched in the sand, struggling to shield her face. This was unlike anything she had ever seen. Sandstorms were common in Autumn Sands, but the strength of this storm was beyond anything she'd ever experienced.

"The horse is a curse!" Amber heard Yris shout, as screams of terror rose up from the background. "It brings the Red Tempest!"

Amber hid her face in her hands. She remembered the conversation she'd heard the night before, about the Desirée wanting to use Shamal's powerful magic. Had they made a grave mistake, turning to the evil horse for help? Was this storm

nature's way of righting things?

The wind intensified, and Amber soon lost sight of everyone and everything that surrounded her. How surprising that people just a few feet away could so easily disappear! She could feel the sand clinging to her face and clothing: It caked onto her mouth and skin. She forced her feet to move, unable to see where she was going or who she was stumbling into. She had to try to find shelter!

She had taken only a few steps when the ground dropped out from beneath her. She felt herself fall. Now she was tumbling, rolling, spinning, dizzy and hurt, unable to see or feel anything but the stinging red sands.

The Red Tempest is going to kill me, she thought as her world dissolved.

CHAPTER

4

*A*mber scrunched her face as something tickled it. She heard a high-pitched laugh, and then another, and another.

Amber brought her hand to her face, brushing sand out of her eyes and blinking awake. *I thought I would die in the sandstorm!* she thought. But her aches and pains told her that she was very much alive. When she opened her eyes fully, Amber could make out several balls of glowing, dancing light—reds, blues, yellows, and greens—against a shadowy background.

She felt a trickle of sand pouring down onto her head. "Sandy!" she heard a squeaky voice cry, followed by more high-pitched, tinkly laughter. "Sandy! Sandy! Sandy!" The trickle increased into a steady stream of sand, and Amber threw her arms over her head to keep more from getting into her hair and eyes.

"Stop it!" Amber cried, quieting the laughter for a moment.

"No sandy!"

"No sandy!"

"No sandy!"

A chorus of the squeaky voices responded, and the stream of sand stopped. Amber squinted as her eyes adjusted to the dim light. She wasn't outside anymore. She seemed to be in some sort of cave. How had she ended up there—and in one piece?

As she looked around, she saw a flock of tiny creatures she had heard stories about before, but never seen: scarab phaeries.

They were small with gossamer-thin wings, a shiny, lacquerlike hide, and broad faces with adorable large eyes and tiny mouths. They were almost as wide as they were tall—making them look surprisingly strong, and very cute. They glowed in a variety of pretty colors.

Scarab phaeries were well known to be mischievous, sometimes maddening, creatures. They were the biggest pranksters in Autumn Sands.

"She wakes!" chirped one excitedly, and the comment was taken up by the others and turned into a chorus: "She wakes! She wakes! She wakes!" But Amber's attention was caught by another noise—something louder than the scarab phaeries' chatter. It came from several feet away, just beyond the phaeries who'd been pranking her with sand.

Amber looked in the direction the sound came from, and felt her heart seize in her chest. *The horse!* It was standing just a few yards from her, free of its restraints. As her eyes continued adjusting to the dim light, she could just make out a few of the scarab phaeries dancing and playing with the ropes that had once held Shamal prisoner. The phaeries must have released him!

"Horse!" Amber heard one of the scarab phaeries chirp beside her. The little phaerie's tone was proud, as though she were showing off a new present.

"Horse!" agreed another phaerie, and a third added something that sounded like "Prince!" But Amber wasn't completely paying attention. Her eyes were still glued to the huge beast. *He is my enemy,* she reminded herself.

Shamal whinnied again and took one cautious step toward Amber. She staggered backward, terrified. Seeming to sense her fear, the horse stopped. Amber refused to make eye contact. She knew what came of that!

"I need to figure out how I got here," she whispered to herself. "And how to get out."

"Out!" cried a scarab phaerie. "No out! Friend!"

"Friend!" agreed another. "Stay! Play!"

Amber sighed and shook her head. "I have to go," she insisted.

Wanting to put more distance between herself and the horse, Amber stood, brushing herself off. She seemed to be in a large, cool cavern surrounded by solid desert rock. There were no entrances or exits that Amber could see. *How did we get in here?* She glanced at Shamal, wondering if he knew, but then quickly looked away.

It doesn't matter. The important thing is finding a way out.

She began prowling, walking the perimeter of the cavern until she found a narrow tunnel leading out. She followed it, twisting and turning, doubling back whenever she came to a dead end, until, at last, she saw a dim red light shining onto the stone walls.

Amber hurried to the end of the tunnel. But she was soon met with a familiar *whoooooosh*ing sound. Then the wind hit her, followed by a wave of stinging sand.

Amber placed her hands over her eyes and stumbled back, ducking into a corner of the tunnel. Cautiously, she peeked outside.

Behind her, she could hear a cluster of phaeries. They had followed her, chattering among themselves.

"Storm!" said one.

"Storm-ly! Storm-ly!" agreed another.

The phaeries were right. The Red Tempest still raged on.

Amber reluctantly made her way back to the large room where the scarab phaeries played and the horse stood on a large flat rock. Careful to leave as much distance as possible between Shamal and herself, Amber settled on the stone floor with a sigh. *I'm trapped,* she thought miserably. *With a horse and these pranksters.*

"Play!" insisted one scarab phaerie, grabbing a piece of Amber's hair and tickling her nose with the ends.

"Play!" agreed another, pulling at Amber's tunic.

Amber sighed. *That storm better be over soon.*

As the hours wore on, Amber tried to doze, but it was difficult with the scarab phaeries tickling her, putting on shadow puppet shows, and pulling at her clothes. The phaeries seemed fascinated by everything about her—her hair, her clothes, her fingernails, even her sandals. At one point, two of the phaeries grabbed a long leather string from her sandals and began forming shapes out of it—stars, flowers, trees.

"Play!" they chattered happily, dancing around her. She could see that another group surrounded Shamal, playing with his mane and tail.

But Amber was in no mood for playing. She wanted to get out of the cave and find the Desirée and the other girls. She hoped that everyone had weathered the storm all right and that they wouldn't travel too far without her. Unfortunately, every time she checked, the wind still howled, and the storm was still in full swing.

Several hours after she first woke, Amber stood at the cave entrance for what seemed like the hundredth time, feeling frustrated. Should she try to brave the storm and go in search of the Desirée? It would be dangerous, but it had to be better than being stuck in a cave with a horse and a bunch of phaeries.

Amber heard a squeak. She looked down by her feet and sighed. One of the phaeries, a tiny red female, had followed her through the tunnel and was perched near her left leg, tugging on her clothes. The phaerie gestured back toward the cavern and then shook her tiny arm toward the storm. "Safe! Cave!" Amber understood what the little creature wanted: for Amber to return to the safety of the cavern. The desert was dangerous at the moment.

Amber sighed in frustration, but allowed herself to be led back down the tunnel. Her stomach rumbled, and Amber wondered when she had last eaten. Was it hours ago? Days? She truly didn't know, but she was ravenous.

Following the phaerie down the twisty tunnel, Amber finally came within sight of the cavern and gasped.

How is this possible?

The far part of the cavern had been transformed into what could only be described as a mini oasis! Palm trees circled a small pool of water, and assorted plants and tropical fruits were suddenly growing in abundance where before there had been only rock! In the middle of the pool stood Shamal. He drank deeply, and Amber could only imagine

how good the cool water must feel going down his throat. Her own throat felt as dry and sandy as the storm outside.

How did this happen? Amber blinked again and again, but the oasis was no figment of her imagination. Her mind raced with questions. Was this a dream? Would she be startled awake as soon as she tried to drink? Had the phaeries conjured this somehow, sensing her hunger? Was it safe?

The phaeries seemed to have none of Amber's reservations about the food and drink, diving hungrily into the tropical fruit.

The red phaerie who had led Amber back to the chamber remained by her side, fluttering about and, Amber realized suddenly, braiding her hair into fancy patterns. "Pretty! Pretty!" chirped the little phaerie.

Amber reached up to feel the phaerie's handiwork and smiled.

Suddenly, her stomach let out a

loud *rrrrowr!* The horse looked over at her, and before Amber could think better of it, they locked eyes. Immediately Amber's mind filled with an overpowering vision of a plumberry, ripe and succulent, shining a gorgeous, unearthly purple. Amber's mouth filled with with saliva. She could eat a plumberry, easily—she just had to walk over and get one from the mysterious oasis.

What did the horse want with her? Was he trying to trick her into eating something poisonous?

Amber's stomach grumbled again. It didn't matter what Shamal's motive was: She was too hungry and thirsty to fight her desire any longer. She stumbled into the oasis, overpowered by the sweet scent of flowers and fruit, and ate and drank until her stomach was bursting.

"Yummy!" cried the red phaerie happily, dancing around Amber's shoulders. "Yummy! Friend!"

When at last she could eat no

more, Amber leaned back into a small area of gravel, her eyelids growing heavy. *I should check on the storm,* she thought, but she felt utterly content where she was. Sighing, she let her eyes flutter closed.

*A*mber wasn't sure how many hours had passed by the time she finally awoke. As soon as her eyes opened, though, she felt a wave of panic. *I have been here for too long. I have to find the other girls and the Desirée.*

She shook her head to clear out the cobwebs and then made her way down the tunnel that led to the cave entrance. Out of the corner of her eye, she could sense the horse and the red phaerie watching her, but she paid them no mind. *They've helped me,* she thought, *but it's time for me to be on my way now.*

Amber let out a sigh of relief when she saw that the desert had returned to normal. The wind was nearly still; the red sands lay in soothing, wavelike patterns. An endless procession of dunes led away from the cave. *I must go.*

Amber returned to the cave to prepare. Her long vest, made of the finest goatskin, provided warmth and protection, but it wasn't strictly necessary for travel through the hot desert. She took it off, carefully forming it into a watertight pouch. She filled the pouch from the oasis before sealing it with a series of knots. Next, Amber took off her filmy tunic and carefully ripped a large piece from the bottom. She took as many plumberries, nectarmelons, and dewy pears as she could hold, and carefully tied them up in her makeshift carrier. She even twisted the corners of the fabric into straps so that she could wear the pack on her back. Sighing, she glanced over at Shamal, feeling his gaze on her. *I won't look into his eyes,* she thought fiercely. The last thing she needed to deal with now was the lure of the equine.

Heaving the fruit onto her back and tucking her water canteen under her arm, Amber ignored the buzzing red phaerie, who flitted around her, chirping "Up! Friend! Up!" The phaerie had been right beside her when Amber awoke, making her wonder if the phaerie had ever left her side. *Oh well,* Amber thought. *I'm sure I was a fun distraction for her.*

Refusing to look back at the horse, Amber began down the tunnel. But she had gone only a few feet when she heard a telltale *clip-clop* on the stone floor behind her. Without turning around, she kept walking toward the exit. The red phaerie flitted beside her, chanting, "Horse! Horse!" in her squeaky voice. Amber ignored her, too.

When they reached the exit to the desert, though, the red phaerie grabbed

Amber's sleeve. "Why? Why?" the phaerie demanded as she beat her wings
wildly.

Amber looked down at her,
stunned to see that the creature was
upset. "I'm leaving," she explained. "I
have to find my group. I lost them in the
storm."

The phaerie shook her head.
"Horse! Horse!" she insisted, just as
Amber heard hooves hitting the floor a
few feet behind her. She turned, meet-
ing Shamal's eyes before she could think
better of it.

Amber was overcome with a vision
of herself leading the horse through
the red desert. Together, they traveled
through the dunes, paused by an oasis
to eat, and camped under the stars. Most
shocking of all was an image of Amber
sitting astride the horse's back as he galloped through Autumn Sands!

"*No!*" she cried, disgusted by even

the thought of such a betrayal of the dune lupine.

Disturbed, Amber pulled her eyes away from Shamal's and charged through the cave entrance, out into the desert. Again the red phaerie tugged her sleeve, shrieking now. "Horse! *Horse!*"

Amber sighed and stopped walking. She knew it was dangerous to travel alone through the desert. And although she didn't trust the horse's motives, he *would* provide protection and possibly assistance during the long journey. Besides, he had been a prisoner of the Desirée. It was probably her duty to deliver him to them again.

Amber turned back and again looked into Shamal's eyes. This time, the horse sent an image of Amber kneeling alone in the sand, stumbling along, clearly exhausted. Then the scene changed, and she was clutching at her throat, sobbing. Amber felt her heart thump with fear.

She knew she could easily end up lost or dying of thirst if she went out into the desert alone.

Amber turned to the horse. "I get it," she said to him with a sigh. "You can come with me, but we are not going to be friends."

The horse whinnied in what seemed like a victorious way, tossing its head and falling into step behind her. The red phaerie squeaked happily, her voice so high-pitched that Amber couldn't make out the words. She had a feeling she hadn't seen the last of this phaerie, either.

"What do you want from me?" Amber asked Shamal a few hours later, as the little group rested under the shade of a lone tree. Not sure where they were now or where the Desirée had been headed, Amber had been forced simply to choose a direction, and she, the horse, and the phaerie had made their way through

the hot sun. The red phaerie had enter-
tained them with silly stories—stories
about clumsy princesses, vain kings,
and kind wanderers. But even as Amber
had chuckled, she couldn't help but feel
uncomfortable in the presence of the
horse, her natural enemy.

Now, she met his eyes. In answer
to her question, he sent her a vision of
himself back in the camp, struggling in
his rope restraints. Then she saw herself,
loosening the ropes.

"Friend," the red phaerie chirped
at Amber, startling her from the vision.
"Friend owes favor."

Amber blinked, looking from the
horse to the phaerie. She couldn't help
but feel a little touched. As soon as the
feeling took root in her heart, though,
she pushed it away, forcing herself to
think about what she was doing. "You're
not my friend!" she insisted. "I could
never be friends with a horse."

Shamal looked down at the

ground, and the little phaerie frowned for the first time since Amber had met her. "Friend," the phaerie insisted. "Horse is your friend!"

Amber blinked, surprised to feel a tear burning the corner of her eye. "He's not my friend," she said again, a little less certain this time.

"Cave!" the red phaerie cried, reaching out to slap Amber's hand. She was so tiny, it felt like barely a pinch, but it stunned Amber nonetheless. "Horse brought you to cave!"

What? Amber looked up, shocked. But . . .

She glanced at Shamal, just for a second and immediately saw an image of herself—unconscious—slung over Shamal's back. He was still bound by restraints, but with no one holding the ends, he was able to stumble through the cave entrance. As soon as he did, he collapsed on the floor, and the phaeries surrounded him—lifting Amber off his back and busily untying his restraints.

He saved me, Amber thought. *The horse saved my life.*

"I . . . ," she said, getting to her feet. She'd already shared some food and water with the horse and the phaerie, and the sun was dipping low in the sky. "I . . ."

She could feel the horse's and phaerie's eyes on her, waiting.

She swallowed. "We have to go," she said finally. She felt more confused and uncertain, but she hoped that when they found the Desirée things would start to make sense again.

mber, Shamal, and the red phaerie slowly made their way through the desert. Ever since it had been revealed that Shamal carried Amber to the cave, the horse had become distant, no longer sending strong images to Amber every time she chanced to make eye contact with him. This was more than okay with Amber, who was still struggling with what she had just learned. Was it really possible that a horse, the sworn enemy of lupines and all who pledged their loyalty to the

Desirée, had saved her life?

Why? What was in it for him? thought Amber.

She couldn't come up with an answer. So instead she focused on survival. Aside from a few conversations with the red phaerie, Amber put her energy into moving through the desert in the hope of eventually finding the Desirée. With the sun as her guide, Amber steered the small group toward what she hoped was the north, where she knew Cavernest lay.

Late in the afternoon, with the sun still blazing hot and high overhead, Amber paused to get her bearings. Were they still headed north? Or had they veered off course somehow? Or . . . did it even matter?

Snnnooort.

Amber jumped, turning to see that Shamal had crept up beside her. For such a huge creature, he was oddly good at that. Amber frowned. "What do *you* want?"

Shamal tossed his head toward the left and then snorted. Giving Amber a long look, he started walking in the direction he'd indicated.

"Hey!" she shouted after him, annoyed. "Where do you think you're going?"

Shamal glanced back at her, snorted again, and met her eyes. He sent her an image of herself still standing in the same spot, half buried by sand, unable to decide which way to go. His message was clear: *You're taking too long.* As Amber's mouth dropped open at his rudeness, he turned and kept walking.

Now Amber was annoyed. She glanced back at the sun, trying to clear her head and figure out where they were. No, she had been right: They *were* headed north. And now Shamal was breaking off to the west!

"Hey, get back here!" she shouted after him. "We're going the right way! Come back!"

Shamal stopped in his tracks, not turning around to look at her. He seemed to hesitate, as though he wasn't sure he could trust her.

"Come *on!*" she cried. "Let's go! On to Cavernest!"

It took a few minutes, but finally Shamal turned back, and the trio continued toward the north.

As the afternoon light grew dim, Amber started looking for a good place to stop for the night. "Where? Where go?" asked the red phaerie when the sun had almost disappeared.

Shamal snorted. Amber sighed, not wanting to look at him. When she finally turned around, Shamal had settled down on the sand, as though he were bedding down for the night. He snorted again, and Amber locked eyes with him and saw a vision of the three of them camping where they were.

"No!" Amber cried. "Not yet! We haven't made enough progress today."

Shamal snorted and looked away. He showed no sign of moving any time soon. Amber paused to take a sip of their dwindling water supply and to give herself time to think. As she reknotted her canteen, she heard the red phaerie squeaking excitedly, "Horse! Horse!"

Amber looked up and found Shamal had moved a few yards away. Now, miraculously, he was standing in the shade of three palm trees. At his feet was a small pool of clear water surrounded by a fringe of dark green grass: a tiny, perfect oasis.

"Oh!" Amber cried, running to Shamal before she could think better of it. "I don't know how you created an oasis out of thin air, but it's amazing."

The horse met her eyes, and Amber had a fleeting but familiar vision of herself loosening Shamal's restraints. Amber had helped Shamal, and now he was helping her.

In spite of herself, Amber felt a

rush of warmth for the horse. "You're a pain sometimes, but I suppose you're all right," she told Shamal.

That night, they drank water from the oasis and shared some of the fruit Amber had brought. Once they'd finished eating, they relaxed around a blazing fire. Staring into the orange flames, Amber thought of her childhood. How many times had she gone camping with her mother? Too many to count. She felt a sharp pain in her heart, wondering when she would see her parents again. To make herself feel better, she began to sing an old campfire song her mother had taught her.

The magic land of Autumn Sands
Always will be free!
The dune lupine and the Desirée
Keep it safe for me!

Amber sensed Shamal watching her, but she kept singing:

The evil horses will never destroy
The things that we hold dear!
We'll make them pay, we'll beat them out,
We'll show them how to fear!

Shamal let out an angry *neigh!* Startled, Amber turned to look at him. He glared at her with such a furious look, it was almost funny.

He shook his head, snorting hard. *Now see here,* he seemed to be saying.

Amber couldn't help laughing. "It's an old song, Shamal," she said simply. "And, anyway, it's the truth. Horses are violent. All my life I've heard terrible stories of cities destroyed and people killed by horses."

Shamal let out another angry snort, and the red phaerie made an odd sound, like a sigh. Amber knew they both disapproved of what she was saying, but she continued anyway.

"What about Ilnut?" Amber challenged, leaning toward Shamal. "My friend told me that horses followed a man home, charged into the city, and burned it to the ground." As she spoke, Amber felt angrier and angrier. How dare this horse try to pretend his kind hadn't been trying to kill hers for centuries?

Shamal looked away into the night and then back at Amber. Her mind was filled with a vision of a man in a small dwelling, writing furiously on a stack of paper. As the man wrote, his arm knocked over his lantern, setting fire to the reams of paper that filled the hut.

Amber gasped. "A man started the fire!" she said, blinking.

Shamal turned away. He snorted once, angrily as he walked a few steps away from the fire, avoiding Amber's eyes.

Amber glanced at the phaerie, who was watching her with a look of disappointment. "Lies," the phaerie said softly, with none of her usual playfulness.

"It was a lie?" Amber asked, still having trouble believing what Shamal and the phaerie were telling her. Was it possible? Had Ruby's whole story been a lie? Had she been told lies all of her life?

It was too much to think about right now. Amber stood and took a sip of water. "I think we should get some rest," she said.

Amber was exhausted, but she slept fitfully, unable to calm her mind. Late into the night, she heard a rustling in the sand. She jumped to her feet and, taking a torch from the fire that still burned low, walked in the direction of the sound she'd heard. There was nothing there.

As soon as she woke up the next morning, Amber checked the spot again. Three sets of dune lupine tracks disappeared into the distance. *We're being followed,* Amber realized, her heart quickening. Her allies, the lupines, had found her—but because she was traveling with an enemy horse, they must have mistaken her for an enemy, too.

As the red phaerie and Shamal prepared to leave the campsite, Amber stared at the dune lupine tracks. *If the dune lupine are nearby, maybe Cavernest is, too,* Amber thought.

Amber was startled by a whinny behind her. She turned to see Shamal and the red phaerie approaching. Shamal's dark eyes were trained on the ground. He had obviously spotted the dune lupine's tracks, too.

The little red phaerie chanted, "Wolf-ly! Wolf-ly!" in what could only be described as an alarmed voice.

"I know," Amber said, trying to be patient. "The dune lupine must be in the area. That means Cavernest may be closer than we think. We must keep moving until we find it."

The group again set off through the desert. Soon the sun shined brightly overhead, and the heat made them all feel exhausted and fuzzy headed. Every so often, they came across tracks of the dune lupine, but there was no sign of the wolves themselves.

As they prepared to break for lunch, Amber realized something. Shamal, who'd fought her so hard on everything the day before, was following along without complaint. She looked at him and saw his eyes trained on the horizon. He seemed tense, even fearful.

Amber bit her lip. Much was at stake for her if the dune lupine caught up with them: She'd been traveling with an enemy horse, and that made her a potential traitor. But Amber knew that the Desirée would likely forgive her. She remembered how they'd reacted when she'd loosened Shamal's ropes. They all knew about the lure of the equine, and they would assume she was just another victim.

But was she?

Suddenly, Shamal let out a sharp whinny. Amber turned to look at him, and followed his eyes to a spot on the dunes in front of them. She felt her heart seize.

Dune lupine.

"Wolf-ly!" the little phaerie cried, shrieking in her already high voice. "Wolf-ly! Danger!"

There were three of them visible, but Amber knew there would be more. They strolled calmly, casually, their graceful gait seeming utterly confident. These were the kings of the desert. *And I am on their side,* Amber thought. Every time she saw the majestic creatures, her heart swelled with pride, and she felt that pride now.

It would take only a second. With one cry, one wave, Amber could summon her allies to her side and be done with this horse forever. She could rejoin the Desirée, begin her Year of Grace, and perhaps even be chosen to bond with a dune lupine cub one year from now.

But . . .

Shamal whinnied softly. Amber

looked at him again and felt herself soften. His dark eyes were trained on hers, but he sent her no visions this time. Shamal simply looked deep into her eyes and allowed her to see the fear he was feeling.

Amber pulled her eyes away. The dune lupine were ahead of them, not behind; that meant they wouldn't see the tiny band of travelers unless Amber called out to them. The wind was blowing down the dune, too—so they wouldn't catch Shamal's scent, because it was being carried away from them.

Amber reached out and touched Shamal's flank, gesturing for him to be still. She turned and caught the red phaerie's eye, drawing her finger to her lips: *Quiet*.

They stood there, frozen, for what seemed like hours, but was probably just a few minutes. Soon, the dune lupine were out of sight, and the desert was silent.

Amber glanced at Shamal. "Let's go," she said finally. "We'd better find somewhere to hide until they're out of the area."

Shamal stared at her, warmth in his liquid brown eyes. Amber knew he understood what she had just done for him—what she could have done to him. He tossed his mane and stamped his feet, sending Amber images of food, water, and shelter. "Are you telling me you know where we can go?" she asked the horse. "Somewhere we will be safe?"

The horse whinnied, nodding, and turned to face the east.

"Lead the way," she urged Shamal.

Once again, the tiny caravan made its way across the desert. This time, they walked toward the east.

CHAPTER

7

After a long day of walking, Amber felt her eyelids grow-ing heavy as the sun dropped low on the horizon. Already the desert breeze was growing cooler, hinting at the cold night to come. The day had been suc-cessful, at least by one measure: There had been no sign of the dune lupines who had tracked them to their camp the night before. Amber hoped it was safe to stop for the night.

"Shamal," she said, "and my little friend"—she looked down at the phaerie, flitting along by her elbow—"let's find a place to stop for the night. The sunlight is fading, and I'm tired."

She looked at Shamal, who threw his head back, whinnying. She was struck by the image of the three of them walking on through the desert—in the darkness.

"Keep going!" the little phaerie insisted, looking between the two of them. "The horse wants."

Amber sighed. "Shamal," she said, "I feel we're safe. We've seen no sign of the dune lupine."

But Shamal simply tossed his head again and continued walking. With a sigh, Amber fell into step behind him.

All right, she thought. *Just one more hour.*

The sun disappeared and darkness fell. In the inky desert sky, the Auraborus lights shined like precious jewels. After what felt like hours, Shamal let out a loud neigh. Turning to look at him,

Amber's mouth dropped open.

Standing before them was the rocky entrance to what appeared to be an underground cave.

Amber carefully approached the dark cavern. The red phaerie flitted behind her, chanting, "Sleep! Sleep!" Shamal seemed to be hesitating for some reason. Amber looked into the narrow passageway. It angled down slightly, leading deep into the ground.

"Let's go," Amber encouraged her friends. "It looks safe. We'll walk slowly and look out for other signs of life."

After building a fire and lighting her torch, Amber led the way into the cave. After a few minutes of walking, her light fell upon a darkened pattern on the cavern walls. She edged closer to get a better look.

Tiny figures were etched into the stone, performing basic tasks like cooking, hunting, and cleaning. Beside several human figures, a larger, four-legged creature seemed to be fetching fruit from a tall tree.

"Is that . . . a horse?" Amber asked, glancing nervously back at Shamal and the phaerie. She was surprised to see evidence of human beings working alongside horses. Weren't horses the enemy? Hadn't they always terrorized Autumn Sands?

Yet again, Amber's beliefs about horses were being challenged.

Behind her, Shamal whinnied softly.

"Horse," the phaerie agreed, her high voice uncharacteristically gentle. "Horse."

Amber frowned. "Someone must have lived in this cave before," she said, "but it seems empty now." Pushing her torch in front of her, she moved forward. Several yards ahead, she could see a faint light—was it a chamber? Was the tunnel opening up, finally?

She walked purposefully down the tunnel, emerging into a larger space and shining her torch around her. At the

sight of what lay before her, her mouth dropped open. Shamal walked around from behind her, leading her way into the room.

"Oh . . . my . . ."

The red stone chamber, which shined a rich, warm orange in the golden torchlight opened out into a beautiful mini city. Crumbled ruins of pillars, arches, and ledges seemed to glow from within, connected by elaborate, but largely collapsed, stone bridges. Intricate drawings and patterns were carved into every pillar and arch. The effect was stunning.

The red phaerie suddenly swooped forward, extinguishing Amber's torch with a wave of her wings. Amber cried out, disappointed to lose the gorgeous city in the overpowering darkness, but the red phaerie chirped: "Lightly! Lightly, friends," and suddenly the city was illuminated by hundreds of tiny colored lights.

"Phaeries," Amber gasped, amazed by their sheer number. There must have been at least three or four times as many as had been in the other cave where she'd met the red phaerie.

Shamal turned to face her, and Amber understood that he had brought her to this place on purpose—he had known it was here.

"Is this your home?" she asked, confused. But no one lived here—the cave city had clearly been abandoned many years ago. "How do you know this place?"

In response, Shamal snorted and moved forward. Amber understood that he wanted her to follow, and she did.

Shamal led her down a steep ramp to what seemed to be the underground city's gathering place. Neatly stacked dwellings, all carved from the cavern walls, surrounded a cleared area that faced a huge stone platform, like a stage. The wall behind the stage was dominated by one huge drawing of an enormous tree. At the top of the tree was written THE CITY OF UPIR.

"Oh," Amber breathed. "This must have been a huge city at some point!" Around her the scarab phaeries twinkled and danced, chanting, "Home! Home!" She wondered what they meant.

Shamal led her to the base of the etched tree and directed his gaze up. Amber followed his eyes.

No, it couldn't be.

On each branch of the tree there was a picture of a horse. Amber looked up and realized, now, that the tree grew wider and wider as it got closer to the stage—she was looking at a family tree! A family tree . . . of *horses*.

"Oh, my," she whispered, looking down from branch to branch. "At one time there must have been thousands of horses in Autumn Sands!" Nothing like it was today, with horses driven near extinction by their war with the dune lupines. She looked at Shamal. He looked down sadly and then back to the tree.

Amber felt her breath catch as her gaze fell on an image in the middle of the tree.

It was Shamal, or a beautiful relative of his. A dark chestnut with a tiny white blaze, white socks, and a jet-black snip. Beneath the picture was the inscription PRINCE SHAMAL I.

"Is that you?" Amber asked.

Shamal tossed his head and then met her eyes, sending her a vision of picture stacked upon picture, ten horses high. At first, Amber was confused, but then it came to her: "He's your great-grandfather, ten times removed?"

Shamal snorted, looking pleased.

"Shamal," Amber cried, shaking her head as she looked at the magnificent horse. "You're a prince!"

Turning back to the wall, she

carefully studied the pictographs—not only the family tree, but the pictures that led in either direction, telling the rich history of this forgotten city. The pictures told of a vital, prosperous place, founded and built by a remarkable line of horses—although it appeared from the pictures that humans had eventually settled there. The horses on the wall looked heroic, powerful, and wise—nothing like the monsters that had crowded Amber's imagination throughout her youth. Some of the horses on the wall even had wings, soaring proudly on the winds, fighting for the honor of their beautiful city.

Suddenly, a low, menacing growl whipped through the silence. Amber felt herself freeze as the reality of what she was hearing hit her. *The dune lupines!* Shamal seemed to melt away, like smoke. One moment, he was next to Amber; the next, he was gone. *How can something so huge move so silently?* Amber wondered, and then realized that she too needed to hide! Leaping into motion, she managed to spring from the stage toward the corridor just as five snarling wolves blocked the only exit.

They studied Amber and Shamal with hate in their eyes, glowing yellow in the dimly lit chamber. Like all the people of Autumn Sands, Amber understood the guttural language of the dune lupines.

"Where is the accursed horse?" they demanded.

8

*A*mber's lip trembled. Everything she had ever been taught told her to tell them where Shamal was and let them recapture the horse. But after the last few days, Amber couldn't help feeling that that would be truly wrong. Shamal was a good, noble creature. He came from royal stock! And he had saved her life more than once.

But did she have the courage to lie to the dune lupines?

The wolves circled Amber. She could tell from their snarling faces that they were becoming impatient.

"*THE HORSE!*" one of them roared. "Where is he? We know he's here. His stink pollutes the ruins of Upir."

Amber took a breath. In, out. She could do this. She *had* to do this.

"He isn't here."

The lead dune lupine, a smoke-colored beauty with chiseled muscles and sharp, glittering eyes, snarled, gnashing his teeth in an angry grimace. "Not here?"

"No," Amber insisted, shaking her head and looking at her feet. "I . . . I don't know where he is. I was traveling with him for a while, yes, but I haven't seen him for . . . at least a day."

The leader moved toward her. Slowly, agonizingly slowly, he circled Amber and then stopped in front of her and sniffed the air dramatically. When he spoke, his voice was low and quiet, scarcely above a whisper. "Then why can I smell him." It wasn't a question.

Amber's chin wobbled as she struggled to speak, but she would not betray Shamal. "He . . . I . . . his scent is in my clothing. Like I said, I traveled with him for some time."

The dune lupine stood back, examining her closely. The rest of the pack watched him carefully, waiting for their cue.

"I smell him," the dune lupine repeated, looking down at the ruined city center. "I will see for myself. Woe to you, girl, if you're lying to us."

Amber stood frozen as the pack of wolves ran around her to get down the ramp to the city. She couldn't see the main square where she'd left Shamal. It was hidden by dwellings and crumbling monuments. She noticed that all but a few of the scarab phaeries had extinguished their glow. They were trying to help Shamal by making him harder to find in the dim light.

Soon she heard the snarls of the

furious lupines, followed by defensive sounds from Shamal.

"The girl is a *liar!*" shouted the head lupine. His growl filled the chamber, and Amber felt her veins fill with fear. By hiding the horse, she had betrayed her own kind. And she knew she would be punished, severely. But she was more worried about Shamal—who knew what they would do to him?

As though released from a spell, Amber forced herself to move again, running down to the main square to find her friend.

Shamal stood on the stone stage. He was surrounded by the dune lupines, who all glared at him, their yellow eyes furious, their teeth bared. Shamal held himself proudly, his head high, his eyes confident. He looked, Amber realized, very much like his royal ancestors in the pictograph behind him.

As Amber approached, the head lupine turned to watch her, anger glowing in his eyes. Amber saw him glance behind her, just for a moment, and she turned and felt her heart sink at the sight of the Desirée filing into the chamber.

Yris was the first to reach the clearing, looking coldly from Amber to the wolves to the horse. "You have found him," she observed, gesturing toward Shamal. She glanced at Amber. "And . . . the girl?"

The head lupine snarled. "She has betrayed us!" he bellowed, his eyes shining with disgust. "She has been traveling with the horse. And she lied to us, telling us he was not here."

Yris turned to face Amber, who gulped nervously. The woman's eyes were completely cold, her expression blank. "Is this true?"

Amber couldn't answer. She looked to Shamal for help, but he could only look back at her with sympathy. They were both caught now.

"Yes," Amber finally forced herself to say. It was the truth. She was on the horse's side.

Yris narrowed her eyes. "Then you will never be one of us. You've been corrupted by the equine. Step out of the way. If you don't, we will know you are our enemy, and we will treat you accordingly."

Amber didn't know what to do. If she stayed where she was, she may be attacked—but if she moved and let them hurt Shamal, she would never be able to live with herself.

"What will you do to him?" she asked Yris, trying to buy time. The wolves growled menacingly, and Amber feared they wouldn't be satisfied with merely recapturing Shamal.

Yris sighed. "If he will allow us to capture him," she explained, "we will take him to Cavernest. There, crops are failing because the underground springs are not as plentiful as they once were. The landscape is changing, child. And to save our city . . ." Her face hardened into a grimace. "We must use the magic of this . . . *horse.*"

Use the magic? Amber thought, confused. "What magic? What do you mean?" she asked.

Yris looked down at Amber with something approaching sympathy. "He has not shown you?" she asked, tilting her head in confusion. "You have traveled with him through the desert, and he has not shown you that he can bring life to the driest parts of the world? He can make water appear at will and replenish starving plants."

Amber looked at Shamal, recognition striking her. The oasis in the cave! She gasped. And the tiny oasis where they had camped the night before, when they found the wolf tracks!

"You!" she cried to her friend, shaking her head in amazement. "You *did* create the oasis in the cave! You saved us, Shamal!"

Shamal neighed and lowered his eyes.

"He is vile and dangerous, but he has his uses." Yris smiled then, a cruel smile. "And as our captive, our slave," she said, enjoying her power over the horse, "we can use his magic while keeping him well restrained."

Amber gulped. *Well restrained?* "You mean for his whole life?" she asked. "You mean—you'll use him forever? Shamal will never be free again?"

Yris glared at her. "He is a *horse*." She insisted. "He does not deserve freedom. If we free him, he will destroy us, as horses have tried to do for generations."

Amber shook her head. "But what if—what if the springs replenish themselves?" she asked. "*Then* will you free him?"

Yris scowled again. "The springs will not replenish themselves," she said simply. "The land is changing, girl. We live in the midst of a desert. From now on, we will need—" She looked at Shamal and grinned that cruel smile again. "A little assistance to survive."

Amber's heart was thudding powerfully in her chest. Yris's explanation seemed to get worse and worse. Cavernest was drying out—but that did not make it right to enslave this noble creature. Amber felt sure that the only reason the city's residents would allow such cruelty, was that the magical creature was a horse, an animal they had been taught from birth to fear and despise.

"That's wrong," Amber said simply to Yris.

But Yris brushed off Amber's words as though she were nothing more than a pesky fly. "If he refuses to come with us," she said, "then the lupines will kill him."

"No!" Amber shouted.

As she said this, Shamal tossed his head and snorted, pawing the ground in front of him. Slowly, he looked from wolf to wolf, making eye contact with each, challenging them. Amber realized what he was trying to tell them: He would not go with them willingly. After getting to know the royal horse, she would have expected no less.

Yris smirked. "The horse means to fight us," she observed, turning back to the rest of the Desirée. They all tittered. "He has no hope of winning, but let him try!"

"I will not allow you to hurt Shamal!" Amber said, sounding braver than she felt.

"Step *aside!*" Yris insisted, grabbing Amber's arm and pulling her out of the center of the ring of dune lupines. "You have proven to us that you will never be one of us, girl. Now allow us to get rid of this evil creature, and we'll deal with you later."

Amber struggled to free herself, but it was no use. Yris held her in an iron grip. The growling and snarling of

the Lupines grew louder, while Shamal danced in a circle, pawing at the ground and snorting just as loudly.

Amber suddenly had a thought.

That was it!

Amber looked behind her and then all around the ruined city. She could no longer see them, but she knew they were there. Watching. And on Shamal's side.

"*Sandy!*" she yelled, as loud as she could. "Sandy! Sandy! Sandy!"

CHAPTER

9

$\mathscr{S}$andy! Sandy! Sandy!"

As the words left Amber's mouth, the chamber was suddenly illuminated by thousands of tiny colored lights. The phaeries were coming to Shamal's aid. They flew toward Amber, their colorful gossamer wings buzzing with motion.

"Sandy! Sandy! Sandy!" they chanted in their squeaky voices.

Within seconds, the chamber was filled with howling wind and sand. The phaeries had conjured a sandstorm in the middle of the chamber. Amber could hear the dune lupines whining, trying to cover their faces with their paws. Amber drew her tunic up around her face, shielding herself from the stinging, pelting sand.

"Scarab phaeries!" shouted Yris furiously. "They have befriended these pests! Arrrgh!"

Pushing through the blowing sand, Amber moved toward Shamal. "Let's go now, while they're struggling!"

But as she finished speaking, the sandstorm intensified. The phaeries were still chanting, "Sandy! Sandy! Sandy!" over and over, and the winds seemed to increase every time. Soon Amber was thrown off balance as the strong currents of sands threatened to knock her over.

"Shamal! Help!" she called out.

She heard a sharp, warning whinny. He was right beside her! "Shamal!" she cried, toppling forward and grabbing on to his strong flank.

The air was suddenly filled with a grinding sound that seemed to be coming from the sky—if they could have seen the sky beyond the chamber roof. Amber and Shamal both looked up, Amber trying to shield herself from the sand with Shamal's mane, and saw that the stone roof was slowly crumbling away, like sand released into the wind. Amber touched Shamal's cheek. "Something magical is happening here," she whispered. "This is our chance to get out of here!"

Just then, there was an ear-splitting *crack*. An electric pulse of magical energy slammed through the room, crackling with red fire, sending the phaeries tumbling in all directions. Immediately, their chant of "Sandy! Sandy! Sandy!" stopped, and so did the sandstorm. Amber blinked, brushing the sand out of her eyes and hair, as the air slowly cleared.

The Desirée and dune lupines had gathered together, and they were blocking the ramp that led to the exit. They had joined forces to produce the powerful magic that had sent the phaeries tumbling. Even now, Yris had one hand on the largest dune lupine and one hand pointed at Shamal. "Next time," she said, a cruel smile spreading across her lips. "I will aim directly at the horse."

Amber felt her stomach sink. She and Shamal were trapped again. Their sandstorm ruse had bought them some time, but not their freedom. And now, more than ever, she was convinced that she did not want to rejoin the Desirée. She was surer than she had ever been that the horse was right and they were wrong. Horses were not evil; they were gentle, noble, and magical.

All her life, she had been aligned with the wrong side.

Shamal snorted and tossed his head, pawing the ground again. Amber could see that he was preparing to fight. Then she felt a tiny tug on her sleeve.

"Amber!" a tiny voice chirped. "Amber! Run! We run with Shamal!"

She looked down. It was the tiny red phaerie, looking at her with large, imploring eyes. "Phaeries stop them!" she promised. "Hold them, hold them. Go!"

Amber felt her heart surge with emotion. "Thank you," she told the tiny phaerie. But even as she said it, she knew those words could never be adequate to express what she felt.

The phaerie nodded with apparent satisfaction. "Friend," she said simply. "Now go. Go-ly, go-ly, go-ly!" she chirped.

Amber looked at Shamal and then at the band of lupine and Desirée that faced them. They were a powerful crew: twelve women, twelve lupine. The lupine were watching them hungrily, growling low in their throats. Amber felt Shamal gently nudge her shoulder with his nose. She turned and saw that he had kneeled

CHAPTER

10

*S*hamal lurched forward, sending Amber tumbling back. She
gasped and grabbed on to his mane.
"Run! Run! Run!" the little red phaerie
cried.

Shamal charged toward the band
of dune lupines and Desirée, not hesitating for even a second. Amber felt
her heart begin to race as they grew
closer, and she could see the murder-
ous looks in the eyes of the dune lupines.
Just before they met the band of rivals,
Amber caught Yris's eye. There was no

low to the ground.

"You want me to ride you," she realized, her breath catching on the second-to-last word.

Shamal nodded. Deep inside, Amber felt herself cringing, but she pushed the feeling back. "All right," she whispered, and threw her leg over the side of the huge horse. He snorted approvingly, gently nudging her into place with his nose, and then turned to face the Desirée. Slowly, he stood. Amber forced herself to be strong. She tangled her fingers in Shamal's silky mane, holding on tight.

The tiny red phaerie landed o Shamal's neck and clutched his man They were ready.

"Okay," Amber told the hor bravely facing the Desirée. "Let's go.'

warmth in that look, only cold, unforgiving anger. Amber shuddered. *I almost became like her,* she realized. *I was on her side once.*

"*Grrrrroooowwwwl!*" The dune lupines sprang forward, their powerful jaws lunging at Shamal's flanks. Amber instinctively pulled her feet upward, leaning forward and digging her knees into Shamal's sides. "Stop!" Yris cried, as they passed through the group, heading for the corridor that led to the desert. "If you go, Amber, you will always regret it! There is no coming back from the evil of the horses. You will have crossed to the other side, once and for all!"

Amber dug her knees deeper into Shamal's side, and he ran even faster. She turned back to Yris, calling, "I have already crossed over!" Then, as the last dune lupine fell off their course, leaping to try to catch Shamal's tail but chomping at air, she said it again. It felt so good. It felt *right.*

"I have already crossed over!"

The dark corridor sped by, and suddenly the three of them were back in the desert, just as they had been all the time they traveled together. This time, though, it felt a hundred times better. Amber took a deep breath, drinking in the pink light of dawn as she soared through the dunes on Shamal's back. A loud thunderclap split the air. Shamal slowed, just for an instant, and Amber turned around to look back at the cave. The cracking sound continued, and then suddenly there was a *whoosh,* followed by another, and another. . . .

Amber gasped.

The cave that had hidden the ruins of Upir was collapsing. Amazingly, though, the heavy stone walls didn't seem to be crashing down on the ruins— instead, they were turning to sand, falling to the ground like rain. And as the cave disappeared, the ruins seemed to rise up into the desert, the broken buildings

poking into the horizon line.

The landscape of the desert had magically changed. The ruined city had returned! Where once there was a sea of dunes, now the city of Upir stood in all its immensity.

Amber looked at Shamal. She could see the pride shining in his eyes, pride at having the beautiful city of his ancestors revealed to the world once again.

"Let's go," she whispered, and he galloped toward the city streets.

The Desirée and dune lupines were nowhere to be seen. Amber wondered what had happened to them. Had they escaped or been buried in sand? She no longer cared, as long as they were no threat to her and Shamal. They galloped through the ruins, along the sandy streets, past more of the stacked dwellings they had seen earlier and huge, gorgeous cathedrals carved from stone.

Shamal paused before the pictograph of his ancestors in the city square. Amber smiled. It remained in perfect condition, untouched by the sandstorm or the cave's collapse.

"Now everyone can learn your noble history," she told Shamal proudly. "Everything changes now. Everything!"

Shamal snorted happily, and then they took off galloping again, the little red phaerie chanting, "Free! Free! Free!"

This is a whole new world for me, Amber thought, as the desert whizzed by. *I've left my home, my culture, my beliefs. I'm not even sure where we're going. And I may never again see my parents.*

It was a scary thought. Amber's whole world had been upturned, and she had no idea what to expect. It was terrifying—but also exhilarating.

Look at what I used to think about horses, she thought, stroking Shamal's mane. *And look how wrong I was. Who knows what else I was wrong about? Anything is possible.*

And that thought filled Amber with hope for the future. If she had been shown the error of her ways, then she could do that for others, too. Maybe she and Shamal had an important job to do: They could help heal the wounds of the past, erase the misunderstandings and mistrust. Maybe they could truly change things for the better.

She smiled and breathed in, the cool air filling her lungs.

Now we are free. . . .

*S*hine Anders placed a beaded bracelet on the velvet-lined shelf. "That's the last one," she announced, closing the glass cabinet. She took a step back and surveyed the shop.

Her heart swelled with pride. Things had certainly changed. Not so long ago, Shine, her mother, and her grandmother were living on the grounds of Rolandsgaard Castle, working as servants for the family of the castle caretaker.

After Shine's father died, they had had terrible trouble making ends meet. But that was before Shine met the legendary horse Jewel. With the beautiful bay mare's help, Shine had found the

Rolanddotter royal vault. Along the way, Shine and her mother had discovered an old jeweler's manual and special tools. For generations the Anders family had been jewel crafters for royalty—all the way back to the days of Sigga Rolanddotter. Now they had their own shop—the Treasure Trove. The Treasure Trove was the beginning of their new life.

"Is everything ready for our grand opening?"

Shine turned to see her mother and grandmother come into the main room of the shop from the back.

"We're ready!" Shine declared.

"Shine, you're sparkling as much as the gems!" her grandmother teased.

Shine's cheeks flushed. "I'm so excited!" She raced to the front door and peered out. "I hope Gertrude gets here soon."

For all eleven years of Shine's life, her doll Gertrude had been her dearest companion. Shine shared all her secrets, fears, and joys with Gertrude, as Shine's mother had, and her mother before her, for many generations. Then an amazing thing happened. When Shine replaced Gertrude's missing eyes with precious gems, the doll came to life! Gertrude explained she was the guardian of the Rolanddotter royal vault. Shine reunited Gertrude with her doll family, for which they were grateful.

And now Gertrude was on her way for a visit!

The Treasure Trove was down a side lane off the main shopping district of Bagatella Market, not far from the Canter Hollow town plaza, so Shine saw only a few people heading out to work or to market. The Anderses couldn't afford anything more central. *Not yet,* Shine thought.

Even so, Shine thought the Treasure Trove was just perfect. Instead of a regular store, the shop took up the first floor of a house. Upstairs were the rooms where Shine, her mother, and her grandmother lived. Out back was a large yard. Large enough, Shine noted, for a stable. She was looking forward to the day when her family could afford to care for a horse properly.

As Shine gazed out the glass door, she noticed the storm was still brewing over Mount Whitemantle. Everyone in Canter Hollow was talking about the odd weather of the last few days. The clouds glowed as if they were lit from within.

"Look at that yellow sky," Mother commented, as she joined Shine.

"Snow on the ground, but warm enough to go about wearing just a light jacket," Grandmother added, gazing out a window.

"I wonder when the storm will finally hit," Mother said.

As if in answer, a thunderclap broke the calm morning quiet. Shine gasped as she watched lightning in astonishing colors crackle across the sky. "Pink! Gold! Blue!" she exclaimed. "I've never seen lightning like that before."

Go to
www.bellasara.com
and enter the webcode below.
Enjoy!

HCP#-DC4X-ZHL7